Walt Disney's

TOBY TYLER

BASED ON THE BOOK "TOBY TYLER"
BY JAMES OTIS KALER

STORY ADAPTED BY
CARL MEMLING

PICTURES BY
MEL CRAWFORD

GOLDEN PRESS
NEW YORK

Pigs ▪ Poster ▪ Peanuts

Once, about fifty years ago, a ten-year-old farmboy became a star performer in a traveling circus. This might never have happened—if it hadn't been for some hungry pigs, a circus poster, and six peanuts.

The boy, whose name was Toby Tyler, lived with his Aunt Olive and his Uncle Daniel on a modest farm near Guilford.

It was a poor year for crops, and Uncle Daniel couldn't afford a hired man. The gray-haired farmer had to work in the fields from the crack of dawn until sundown. And Toby helped him with the chores.

One morning, Toby vaulted the fence behind the barn on his way to the cow pasture. As the short sturdy boy trotted through the barnyard, a flock of clucking chickens scurried out of the way. Old Red, the plow horse, looked up from the water trough and nickered at him. Toby waved a friendly greeting, but did not stop.

As he neared their pen, the pigs raised their snouts and filled the air with complaining squeals of hunger. But the farmboy went on his way toward the barn.

"Nope," he thought. "Not now. Before I feed those pigs their slop, I've got to put the cow to pasture. And then I've got to . . ."

But Toby never got to finish listing his chores, for just then he turned the corner and saw the poster.

He stopped, his eyes wide with wonder. Someone had slapped the poster up with paste on the front of the barn. Blazing with color against the weathered planking, it said:

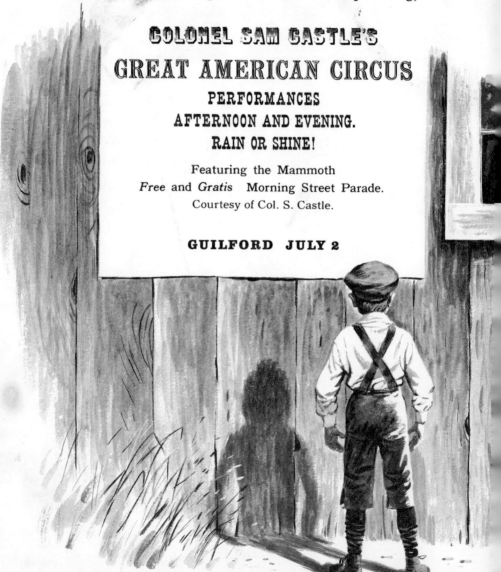

COLONEL SAM CASTLE'S
GREAT AMERICAN CIRCUS
PERFORMANCES
AFTERNOON AND EVENING.
RAIN OR SHINE!

Featuring the Mammoth
Free and *Gratis* Morning Street Parade.
Courtesy of Col. S. Castle.

GUILFORD   JULY 2

Toby's head swam. He brushed his hand across his eyes and stared harder.

"July second," he whispered. "That's today. Guilford . . ."

Then, forgetting the cow, the hungry pigs, and all his other chores, he ran down the road to town.

At Guilford, the parade had already started. When Toby came dashing into town, he could hear music and see nodding plumes and the tops of passing wagons. But the townsfolk were packed so tightly along the narrow sidewalk, they blocked everything else from his view.

Toby took a deep breath and, plunging into the crowd, began crawling between people's legs. At last he managed to fight his way up front. And there he stood, his round face beaming with delight, until the steam calliope that marked the end of the parade came rolling down Main Street.

Toby's next stop was the circus grounds. There he wandered along the midway staring at the large posters in front of the side shows.

A ticket seller called, "Step this way, folks! Get your tickets for the big show here! Count your change before you leave the ticket window! Hurry, hurry, hurry!"

Fishing around in his pocket, Toby came out with one penny. He looked at it ruefully. He hadn't even bought a ticket—but this was all the change he had to count. Sighing, he returned it to his pocket.

Then he stopped to watch a man working inside a booth. The man was flashily dressed, and had crafty eyes. As he filled a tray with striped bags of peanuts, he called:

"Crispy, crunchy, circus peanuts! Get them here!"

Toby had begun fingering the coin in his pocket again when suddenly the man looked up and said, "You a buyer or a looker?"

This was no easy decision for Toby to make. He thought it over for almost a full minute. At last he said, "How many peanuts could I get for a penny?"

The man made a quick mental calculation, then said, "I daresay I could part with, oh, about six."

"Only six?"

"That's *more* than you'd get if you bought them by the bag!" The man's voice rose hoarsely. He seemed grieved that the boy should doubt his generosity. "And *that's* a sober fact."

Again Toby took his time thinking it over. But finally he drew his fist out of his pocket, laid the penny on the counter, and said gravely, "Six peanuts, please."

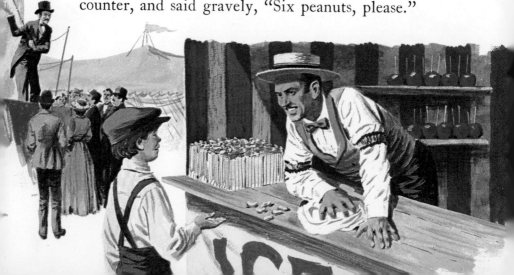

The Golden Opportunity

Toby cracked the first peanut, then made a sour face and said, "You swap the ones back that are bad?"

The man was shocked. "Bad? I don't sell bad peanuts, boy."

"It *tastes* bad."

After glancing about to see if anyone else had heard, the man said quickly, "Here's two more. Now run along. You'll miss the best part of the show."

Toby carefully cracked another peanut. "I'm not going to the show."

"Not going? You lack the price of a ticket?"

"Yes, sir."

"I suppose your parents are bringing you tonight."

"No, sir. I don't have any parents."

"Orphan boy, eh?" Suddenly the man seemed very interested. Leaning forward on the counter, he said, "Ever think of joining a circus, lad?"

"Me?" Toby was so startled, he almost choked.

"Yes, you. Imagine—being part of the glorious family of artists under the big top. Imagine—traveling the length and breadth of this great land of ours . . ."

"But what could I do?" Toby said, bewildered.

"You can become a concessionaire! Like me!"

"I could? A-a . . ." The boy couldn't even pronounce the word.

"Free transportation," the man went on, "a snug place to sleep, all you can eat, see the performance any time you please! And if that weren't enough—each Saturday night, yours truly, Harry Tupper, will present you with one of these!"

Mr. Harry Tupper held up a silver dollar that glinted in the sunlight. "What do you say, boy—is it a bargain?"

Gosh! Toby thought. Working for a circus!

"I guess I'd like that better," he said dreamily, "than anything in the world."

Mr. Tupper chuckled. "You would, eh?"

"Trouble is," Toby continued, "Uncle Daniel and Aunt Olive need me—"

Mr. Tupper's silver dollar quickly flew back to his pocket. Drawing back coldly, he said, "Aunt and uncle—?"

"They're awful poor," Toby said. "And there's lots of work I have to do for them around the farm. But I could ask them maybe—"

Mr. Tupper was no longer interested. "Don't give it another thought," he said. "I'll pick up a boy in the next town. Plenty of them would be glad to get such a golden opportunity."

He dismissed Toby with a wave of his hand and turned back to his work. But when he looked up a few moments later, the boy was still standing there.

Sighing, Mr. Tupper produced his wallet and took out a piece of paper, which he signed with a flourish.

"Just so's we part the best of friends," he said. "Here's a free pass to the performance tonight. Come and enjoy yourself, courtesy of Harry Tupper."

Toby's eyes shone with joy all the way home. He could hardly believe his luck. The piece of paper in his hand was a genuine free pass to the circus!

But when he got to the farmhouse, a spare, graying man with stern features grabbed him roughly by the collar—and the joy drained quickly out of him.

"Where have you been?" Uncle Daniel wanted to know.

Toby flinched. Uncle Daniel's eyes were blazing.

"I-I'm sorry," Toby stammered. "I meant to come back, Uncle Daniel. But there was a parade—and then I happened to go to the circus grounds—"

"Circus!" Uncle Daniel shouted. "Did you know the

pigs broke down the fence because you forgot to feed them —and rooted up the turnip field? *Did* you?"

Toby could only shake his head.

"You're a shiftless, ungrateful boy!"

Aunt Olive moved forward. The middle-aged farm woman spoke softly, trying to calm her husband. "Daniel, don't be so hard on Toby. Boys get skittish when a circus comes to town."

"Toby doesn't have a right to behave like other boys!" the farmer shouted. "Toby's got no right at all—and he knows why."

At this, Toby hung his head to hide the tears that had come to his eyes.

"My wife and I go without things so that we can feed and clothe you," the farmer went on. "I'm a poor man, yet I took you in when no one else would have you. You're no kin to us—you're nothing to us but a millstone around our necks."

Thrusting Toby toward the hall staircase, he said, "Go up to bed and stay there. There'll be no place at supper for you tonight."

When Toby was gone, Aunt Olive said, "Daniel, you were overly harsh with the boy. It's true he let the pigs go hungry—and we've lost our turnip crop. But those were terribly cruel things to say to him. You couldn't have meant them."

Toby didn't hear his aunt. As the sobbing boy trudged up the stairs, a plan was forming in his mind.

He'd wait until dark. Then he'd run away to take advantage of the golden opportunity that Mr. Tupper had offered him. Uncle Daniel would never have to go without things to feed and clothe him again.

14

Runaway

The evening performance was over, and the work of taking down the canvas had started. The circus lot was a bedlam of activity. Torches cast eerie shadows over straining horses and shouting men. Somewhere in the darkness, a tiger roared.

Harry Tupper was loading boxes onto a baggage wagon, when he heard a small voice.

"Here I am, Mr. Tupper," it said.

Tupper looked about. Behind him stood a boy carrying a bundle of clothing.

"Well," Tupper said sourly. "What of it?"

"Don't you know me? You said I could work for you."

The concessionaire put down a box and peered suspiciously at Toby Tyler. "What about that aunt and uncle?"

"It's all right." Toby said huskily. "They don't want me. They said I was a millstone around their necks."

Tupper turned back to his loading. "Then you got a job. Fifty cents a week."

"You said a dollar."

The man glared, but the boy stood his ground.

Finally Tupper shrugged. "If I said a dollar, I meant a dollar. But don't you try running away after I spend my time teaching you the business."

"Oh, no, sir," Toby said earnestly.

Again the concessionaire tried to get back to his loading. This time, Toby said, "Mr. Tupper, I didn't have any supper tonight."

Muttering angrily, Tupper scrambled around in a provision box and came up with a battered looking banana.

"Here you are," he said. "Nutritional gold from the Indies. See that it holds you till morning. Now stay here and keep out of trouble. I'll be right back."

With a sigh, Toby moved near one of the animal wagons and prepared to bite into the mouldy fruit. But just then a small hairy fist darted out through the bars and snatched the banana away.

Whirling quickly, Toby thrust his hand into the cage to seize the paw of a young chimpanzee. As Toby struggled to bring him close to the bars, the chimp gulped down the banana hastily.

"You thief!" Toby cried. "Give that back."

The chimp set up a violent outcry. This touched off a chain reaction of noise from the other monkeys in the cage. And a burly, powerful man came running.

The burly man was Ben Cotter, who doubled as the circus strong man and driver of the monkey wagon. "What did you do to that chimp?" Ben Cotter wanted to know.

Toby was outraged. "*Me?* I didn't do *anything*. It was

16

the monkey. I had a banana and he stole it from me!"

Then Harry Tupper came running. "I thought I told you to stay out of trouble," he shouted at Toby.

"*He* stole my banana!" Toby said.

At this, the chimp gave vent to a new series of cries. And now Colonel Castle, the circus owner, came galloping.

"What's going on here?" Colonel Castle called sharply from the saddle.

Tupper was suddenly all smiles. "Nothing, Colonel. Nothing at all. The monks just got a little excited."

The colonel pointed at Toby. "Who's this?"

"He's my new helper, sir."

The colonel scowled. "Picking them kind of small, aren't you, Tupper?"

"It's all right, sir. He doesn't have any folks, poor lad." Then, stepping forward and lowering his voice, Tupper said, "I planned to take him under my wing—give him a helping hand—"

The colonel snorted. "Spare me your kind intentions, Tupper. Let's get this circus moving. The boy can ride up on top with Ben."

Ben Cotter let out a bellow of protest. "Thunderation, Colonel! Why pick on me to nurse Tupper's sniveling brats?"

"Trim your wagon," the colonel said, cutting him short. "We're moving." Then he wheeled his horse about and rode off.

A few moments later, Ben Cotter was glaring fiercely down at Toby from the driver's seat of the monkey wagon. The boy stirred uneasily. He was glad he was still on the ground. Suddenly he felt homesick. He was just about to tell Mr. Tupper that he had changed his mind about the job, when suddenly the colonel's voice rang out, "*Move 'em!*"

At once the night was alive with the creaking sound of moving wagons. Harry Tupper grabbed Toby and boosted him toward Ben Cotter, who fished him up easily and sent him sprawling over the seat.

Then Ben Cotter snapped the reins, and the wagon started with a jolt.

Toby was clinging desperately to the seat, having all he could do to keep from pitching to the ground, when he heard Tupper call after him:

"You'll be snug as a mouse up there, lad. Ben will be glad to take care of you."

Almost an hour passed before the driver even spoke to Toby. "Let's get one thing straight," he said. "Me—I don't like kids. Especially runaways. They're a weak-livered lot."

Toby said nothing, but his jaw firmed.

"A kid has a good home," the driver said. "First time some little thing goes wrong—he runs away. Then he finds things don't suit him just right — he wants to run home again."

Toby stared at the road, as if measuring the distance there from the wagon seat.

Ben Cotter said, "Go ahead—jump! Nobody'll miss you. I doubt if you're worth missing."

Toby glared, but remained silent.

"Jump! Don't be scared!"

"I'm not scared," Toby said angrily. Then, after a pause, "I'm not scared of you either."

Ben's expression didn't change. "Fair enough, sonny."

"Don't call me 'sonny.' My name's Toby Tyler."

"All right, sonny. We'll call you Toby."

There was another pause. Finally Ben said, "It's none of my business—but maybe you better catch some sleep. Morning comes early with this outfit."

"Not sleepy," Toby said stubbornly.

"Suit yourself."

Defiantly Toby opened his eyes wide, folded his arms across his chest, and stared straight ahead.

The circus caravan, with its line of swinging lanterns, kept moving through the night.

Circus Morning

Toby was awakened the next morning by a small twig landing on his nose. He had been sleeping at the base of the wagon, warmly wrapped in Ben Cotter's coat.

He opened his eyes and looked around, puzzled. Another twig came flying and hit him on the head. Toby sat up, and saw the same mischievous little chimp grinning at him. Glaring angrily, the boy reached to the ground for something to throw.

"You better be up and doin', boy, before Harry Tupper comes looking for you."

Ben Cotter was standing over him, a towel flung over his muscular shoulder. Quickly Toby drew back his hand.

"Thanks for taking care of me last night," he said. "Guess I fell asleep."

"Didn't mean nothing to me one way or another," Ben said gruffly. "I didn't want you falling off—and me getting blamed for it."

Toby looked hurt. "I won't bother you any more."

"I'm sure glad to hear that," Ben said.

The circus camp was pitched and already humming with activity. Men were hurrying back and forth, grooming the animals or working with pieces of equipment. As Ben made his way between carts, stock animals, and crates, Toby followed at a safe distance.

He caught up with the driver at the bank of a small stream and said lamely, "I was wondering where to wash."

Ben pointed at the the stream. "That's water, ain't it?"

"Yessir."

"All right. Now do me a favor and keep out of my way."

Ben moved downstream and began sloshing water on his face. Toby had just squatted down on the bank and was preparing to wash, when an angry voice blasted in his ear.

"What's the idea making me chase all over camp for you?" Harry Tupper wanted to know.

"Morning, Mr. Tupper," the boy said politely. "I was just washing up."

Tupper took him roughly by the arm and began pulling him away. "Not on my time, you aren't!"

Toby stumbled and fell, but Tupper yanked him to his feet again. "Come on! Move along! There's work to be—"

The concessionaire never finished the sentence. For suddenly Tupper found himself lifted off the ground. He squawked with fright.

"*Let me down!*" he screeched.

Ben Cotter had come up behind him, taken him by the shirt slack, and lifted him aloft. Now the strong man was walking back toward the stream, holding Tupper at arm's length as easily as if he were a baseball bat.

"Now, Mr. Tupper," Ben said, "I don't believe in cod-

22

dling—but I got my fill of your mistreating your helpers
before breakfast every morning."

Tupper's feet kicked wildly. "The boy works for me!
I'll do as I like with him!"

Ben went on gravely. "If the boy don't do what you tell
him, Mr. Tupper, you can fire him. But if I ever catch
you roughing him up again, I'm liable to do something like
this—"

Abruptly letting go, Ben dropped Tupper into the
stream. Then he turned and glowered at Toby. "As for you
—listen to Mr. Tupper—work hard and do your job right."

Toby nodded vigorously. "Yessir."

"Now you can go to work soon's you've had your breakfast. The cook tent is over there."

"Yessir."

In the cook tent, a number of performers were seated at planked tables, eating breakfast. Toby came off the chow line, his plate loaded with sausage, scrambled eggs, wheat cakes, and chunks of corn bread. He glanced about uncertainly, not knowing where to sit.

"Why don't you sit over here?"

Toby turned. A little girl was smiling at him. She was the prettiest girl Toby had even seen.

He sat down beside her. Then, remembering his manners, he took off his cap and said, "Thanks."

"My name's Jeanette," she said. "I'm a bareback rider. You're new around here, aren't you?"

"Yes, ma'am," Toby said.

"I ride as a team with Ajax," she continued. "He's twelve years old, and he thinks he knows everything."

Just then a tall boy approached the table. He stared at Toby with annoyance.

"You're not supposed to sit here, you know," he said brusquely. "This is a performer's table."

Jeanette made a face. "Stop it, Ajax. I asked him to sit down."

Not knowing quite what to say, Toby smiled nervously

24

and continued eating. The tall boy pounded the table with his fist. "Did you hear what I said? And look at me when I talk to you!"

Jeanette tossed her head angrily. "Oh, Ajax—let him alone!"

"He's not supposed to be at our table!" Ajax shouted. He pushed Toby. "Go on—get away."

A tall, cheerful-looking man had stopped near the table to watch the quarrel. He moved forward balancing five plates of food along his arm and smiling broadly.

"Well, well—there you are, my boy!" he said to Toby. "Colonel Carter especially asked me to look out for you!"

Toby blinked, puzzled. "Me?"

The man went on smoothly. "Are you taking a professional 'nom de plume' this year—or do you plan to use your own name?"

Toby was bewildered. "My own, I guess—"

"Which is—of course—?"

"Toby Tyler."

"Toby Tyler—to be sure!" the man cried. "Wonderful name! I've always liked it!" Then, turning to Jeanette and Ajax, "You've heard of Toby Tyler, of course."

Now it was Ajax's turn to be confused. The arrogant boy said nervously, "Gosh, if he'd only told us—"

"Tut, tut," the man said. "Too late for apologies." Then, respectfully addressing Toby, "Will you do me the honor of having breakfast with my family and me?"

As they left the cook tent together, Toby's rescuer said, "Allow me to introduce myself. I am Sam Treat, circus clown."

Toby gasped. "A clown?"

Still balancing the plates of food along his arm, Sam Treat bowed. "At your zurvice!" he said in a comical Dutch accent. Then, saluting broadly, he pretended to jab himself in the eye. "Ow!"

When they reached his tent, the clown set the plates along a table and said, "Sit down, Toby. The kids will be glad to see you."

Toby asked, "You have a big family, Mr. Treat?"

"Depends. Most of the time—I'd say—oh, somewhere between four and five." Cupping his hands to his mouth, Sam Treat called, "Hey, kids! Breakfast!"

At this, the lids of four small wardrobe trunks flew open. A pack of dogs climbed out and made a dash for the table. Gathering along the bench on either side of Toby, they fell hungrily on the food.

When Toby could stop laughing, he said, "Gosh, when you said you had a family, I thought—"

Toby paused, embarrassed.

"That's all right," the clown said gently. "They're family to me. Not what you're used to, I suppose."

Toby hung his head. "I don't have a regular family either. That's why I joined the circus."

"That so?"

"I ran away," Toby explained. "It wasn't 'cause they didn't want me. But they're awful poor. I was just a millstone around their necks."

"You figure you'll ever go back?"

Toby heaved a great sigh. "Guess not. Leastways, not till I earn enough money to bring home. So I can show I'm not what they said I was."

While the boy picked moodily at his food, the clown got up and went over to his makeup box. He rooted around in it until he came up with an old, leather money pouch.

Tossing the pouch down on the table, he said, "Save your money in this, Toby. Don't wait till it's too late."

Toby reached for the pouch and held it tightly. "Thank you, Mr. Treat," he said. "I'll work real hard. I'll do everything Mr. Tupper tells me. I'll—"

Suddenly the boy clapped his hand to his head. "Oh my gosh!"

"What's the matter?"

"I forgot about Mr. Tupper waiting for me!"

Toby ran quickly out of the tent, calling back over his shoulder, "Thanks, Mr. Treat! Bye!"

Mr. Stubbs

The afternoon performance was under way, and Toby Tyler was inside the big tent at last. He moved slowly along the aisle, a big tray of peanut bags and taffy apples strapped to his shoulders.

"Peanuts!" Toby called. "Nice crispy, crunchy peanuts and taffy apples! Peanuts! Nice . . . crispy . . . crunchy . . . peanuts . . ."

The words died out slowly on his lips. His head tilted back and his eyes widened. He stood this way, watching the performers on the trapeze at the top of the tent, until suddenly Harry Tupper came up behind him and gave him an angry shove.

Startled, Toby ran off shouting at the top of his lungs, "Peanuts! Peanuts and taffy apples!"

After that, Toby kept his mind on business for almost ten full minutes. But then he heard Colonel Castle announce from the center of the ring,

28

"Ladies and gentlemen! Your kind attention! The Great American Circus presents—the Mighty Banjo!"

Toby paused, his eyes shining as he gave his "kind attention." The Mighty Banjo was Ben Cotter wearing tights.

Proudly nudging a spectator, Toby pointed to the ring and said, "He's a friend of mine."

But then, looking along his pointing finger, he saw Harry Tupper down near the edge of the ring, glaring balefully up at him.

Toby leaped into action at once, breaking out in full cry. "Peanuts! Taffy apples! Peanuts!"

All through the dancing elephant act, the jugglers, the Liberty horses, and the clowns—Toby tended to business.

But then, after a roll of drums, the band broke into a Strauss waltz. Jeanette and Ajax made an imposing entrance, leading their horses into the ring.

Standing directly in front of an indignant spectator, Toby watched them, his mouth slack with awe.

"Down in front!" the specator cried. "Sit down!"

Without thinking, his eyes still on the ring where the two young performers were cantering about gracefully, Toby sat down.

Someone slid into the seat beside him, and a harsh voice grated close to his ear. "Great show, isn't it?"

Toby nodded dreamily. "Sure is."

Still dreamy-eyed, Toby turned to see who shared his own high opinion of the show. It was Harry Tupper, glaring at him more peevishly than ever.

No arrow ever flew from any bow faster than Toby Tyler did from that bench. And for the rest of the performance, he managed to keep his mind on business, and his back to the performers.

29

After the show, Toby went to the lemonade stand and handed over the day's receipts to Harry Tupper.

The concessionaire counted greedily. "A dollar-thirty-five, forty, fifty, sixty, sixty-five—"

Stopping, he held up one coin that shone dully and was softer than the rest. "What's this?" he said. "Why—you blithering greenhorn! Don't you know any better than to take a lead slug?"

"I'm sorry, Mr. Tupper," Toby said. "I don't know much about money."

Tupper snorted. "Then I'll teach you. Lesson Number One—I'm replacing this slug with a nickel out of your first week's pay."

"Yessir," Toby said brightly. Then he held out three nickels. "And what do I do with *these?*"

Tupper scowled. "Where'd you get them?"

"They were left over. When I tried to give them back —they said, 'Keep the change.' "

The concessionaire gulped, startled by the boy's innocence. Then, smiling craftily, he said, "That, my lad, is called a 'tip.' As a matter of custom, all 'tips' belong to the head concessionaire—which is me."

Toby was crestfallen. "Yessir."

"However, if you report *all* your tips, I'll split them with you. Thus—two nickels for me—one nickel for you."

Toby beamed. "Thank you, sir."

Tupper studied him carefully for a moment. Then, satisfied that the boy was fooled, he gestured toward a small mountain of glasses and bowls on the counter.

"Now get busy and clean up that mess," he said. And lighting a cigar, he drifted off.

Toby was tired, but he went right to work clearing the

counter. He took the tray of peanuts and taffy apples, and placed it on top of a barrel near the animal wagon. Then, with a sigh, he went off to get an apron.

After a moment, a chimpanzee's hand reached out from inside the wagon.

The hand groped around until it came to rest on top of a taffy apple.

Then it took hold of the stick.

And then the tray had one taffy apple less than before.

Toby returned with an apron around his waist. An hour later he was polishing the last of the glasses. He proudly set it on the counter next to the rest of the clean shining glassware.

Just then an apple core hit him on the head. Puzzled, he picked it up and looked at it. A second apple core came flying and knocked over a couple of glasses.

Toby hurried over to the barrel where he had left the tray. It had fallen to the ground. Angrily, Toby looked up at the monkey cage.

The little chimp was seated inside the cage amid a pile of peanut shells, torn peanut bags, and remnants of taffy apples. He was nibbling half-heartedly at the last apple when he saw the boy. Snickering, he tossed the apple core feebly at Toby.

Toby sputtered with fury. "You—you—all because of you, Mr. Tupper will skin me alive! I hope you get sick! I hope you get so sick, you turn green!"

That night, the moaning chimp was stretched out on the table in Sam Treat's tent. Toby, Sam, and Sam's family of dogs were all staring gravely down at him.

"He's awful sick, isn't he?" Toby said.

"Don't look so good," Sam said. "That's a fact."

Toby's mouth trembled. "Gosh, I didn't want him to get *this* sick. It's all my fault."

"He'll eat anything," Sam said. "I think he's part ostrich."

Leaning over, the clown reached down toward the chimp's throat and began handing objects back to Toby.

"See what I mean?" he said. "A button hook...a trunk key...a hair brush...a piece of clothesline..."

At first Toby couldn't believe his eyes. When he finally realized that the clown was doing a sleight of hand trick, he grinned with relief.

"Sure had me fooled," Toby said. "Can you fix him up?"

"Always have," said Sam Treat. He reached into a packing case and brought out a jug marked CASTOR OIL.

At sight of the jug, all the dogs vanished into their carrying cases. The chimp tried to squirm off the table, but Toby held him tightly.

"Hang on!" Sam said. "Don't let him bite you!"

As the oil went down his throat, the chimp struggled violently. But then his eyes glazed and the fight went out of him.

Toby gently gathered him up in his arms. The chimp snuggled against the boy's shoulder like an infant, whimpering softly.

32

Toby had a lump in his throat so big he was unable to swallow it. At last he said, "Sure hate to put him back in that monkey cage."

Sam nodded. "Be a good idea to keep him warm tonight. Here—wrap him in this shawl."

"Maybe he can sleep with me," Toby said.

"You better ask Ben," Sam said. "The monks are his responsibility."

When the circus moved out that night, the chimp was still in Toby's arms.

"We're going to be friends now, aren't we, Mr. Stubbs?" Toby said.

"Stubbs?" Ben Cotter said, as he swung up beside Toby on the front seat of the monkey wagon. "Why Mr. Stubbs?"

"He reminds me of old Mr. Stubbs who runs the general store back home."

Toby smiled down at the chimp in his arms.

"Yessir, Mr. Stubbs," he said softly. "Real good friends. That's gonna be us."

Ben snapped the reins, and the wagon lurched forward.

"How I let you talk me into this, I don't know," he grumbled. "Colonel Castle's number one rule is animals stay in cages where they belong!"

Fireworks

Without taking his eyes from the road, Ben reached over and shook Toby awake. The boy yawned and squinted up at the sun. The chimp on his lap was still asleep.

"What time is it?"

"Late," Ben said. "We had a breakdown during the night. We're parading straight into Woodvale, and we'll set canvas afterward."

Toby sat up excitedly. "Gosh — I get to ride in the parade!"

Ben handed him a visored cap and said, "Here—you want to be circus—*look* circus!"

"How about a hat for Mr. Stubbs?"

"Never mind that. Whatever you do, just hang onto that monk!"

As they approached Woodvale, they heard the popping of firecrackers.

"Hey! I almost forgot!" Toby said. "It's the Fourth of July!"

Ben frowned. "Yeah—the animals will just *love* the fireworks!"

Turning up Main Street was like entering an artillery barrage. Mr. Stubbs chattered with fright and struggled in Toby's arms. The horses reared and stomped nervously.

34

A lighted string of firecrackers flew through the air and landed on the monkey wagon, just behind Ben and Toby. When the string went off, exploding violently, Mr. Stubbs shot straight up into the air and made a panicky four-paw landing on the back of one of the horses.

Screaming shrilly, the horse pitched and reared. His terror spread to the rest of the team, and they broke into a wild run. Ben pulled the reins with all his strength, but soon the wagon was tilting dangerously.

"Look out, Toby!" Ben shouted. "Jump!"

Ben rolled clear of the crashing wagon, but Toby had to be pulled away by spectators. Nobody had to help the monkeys. The accident had sprung a door in their cage; and they streamed out and scampered off in every direction, happy to be free.

Toby rose shakily to his feet. He heard Colonel Castle shouting orders. He saw a clown run by with a recaptured monkey under his arm.

Suddenly Toby's face went white. Where was Mr. Stubbs? Was he hurt? . . . Toby ran down the street, searching for his friend.

His friend was in the sheriff's office. The chimp stood on the desk, curiously inspecting a revolver. The muzzle

35

kept swinging aimlessly. It was pointing toward an open window when suddenly the chimp's finger found the trigger.

BLAM! A bullet shattered a street lamp.

BLAM! A plate glass door bit the dust.

News of the gun-toting chimp spread through town like wildfire. Soon Toby came running.

"Look out!" the sheriff called. "Take cover!"

Pulling Toby down, the sheriff made him flatten himself on the ground. "The monk's got just one more shot," he said. "All we have to do is wait him out."

After the next shot, the sheriff grinned with relief. "Rest easy, folks!" he called. "That was the last bullet."

The sheriff rose and dusted off his pants. He was ready to take over his place of business again.

But inside the office, Mr. Stubbs had just found another revolver. And when the sheriff walked calmly through the door—BLAM—a bullet sent his hat flying from his head. The sheriff dived for the street, leaving Mr. Stubbs still in charge.

Now the sheriff borrowed a rifle and drew a bead on the chimp through the window.

"No!" Toby cried. "Please don't hurt him."

"Look out, boy! I hate to do this—but I'm going to get him before he shoots someone," the sheriff said grimly.

But before the sheriff could take aim again, Toby ran for the office.

As the boy came in, the chimp turned quickly, the revolver muzzle swinging with him.

The boy paused. "Hi—Mr. Stubbs," he said. "It's me— Toby." Cautiously, Toby moved closer.

"We're friends now, Mr. Stubbs. Remember?"

36

The revolver weaved erratically. The boy inched forward another step.

"Easy. Eaaasy, Mr. Stubbs."

Toby was still coming forward, his hand held out. Suddenly the chimp turned the gun around, sniffed it, and put the muzzle to his mouth.

"No, Mr. Stubbs! Stop!"

As Toby lunged forward to grab it the gun went off. The bullet thudded into an overhead beam, and Mr. Stubbs jumped into Toby's arms.

Late that night, Colonel Castle showed a newspaper to Ben and Toby. The headlines said:

MONKEYS CAPTURE WOODVALE!
ANIMALS CELEBRATE INDEPENDENCE DAY BY MAKING BREAK FOR FREEDOM!
BOY DISARMS GUN-TOTING CHIMPANZEE!

The colonel beamed at the strong man and the boy.

"Well, it's been quite a day," he said. "Those runaway monks have given us the best business we've had all season."

Then he placed his hands on Toby's shoulders. "Seems like you handle that chimp pretty well. How would you like to take care of him? Try to keep him out of mischief?"

Toby was radiant. "You mean it, sir?"

"You heard me, boy," the colonel said. "From here on in, that chimp is your responsibility."

A Bad Fall

The next few weeks passed very quickly.

Toby and Mr. Stubbs were now a regular feature of the street parade. Each day the boy grew fonder of the mischievous little chimp, but keeping him out of trouble was no easy job. Between watching after Mr. Stubbs, and working for Mr. Tupper—Toby Tyler was kept quite busy.

But he never forgot Aunt Olive and Uncle Daniel. All the money he earned went directly into the pouch given him by Sam Treat. As soon as the pouch got full enough to bring to his uncle, Toby meant to go home.

Then, one day, he paused by the practice ring to watch Jeanette and Ajax.

With her horse still in motion, the tiny girl dropped lightly to the tanbark and came forward to greet him.

"Hello," she said. "We haven't seen you around lately."

Toby smiled shyly. "Mr. Tupper kind of keeps me going."

At that moment Ajax sauntered over. "Well, if it isn't the Great Peanut Salesman!" he sneered. "The Death Defying Daredevil of the Lemonade Stand."

Toby was staring at the practice ring. "Sure are pretty horses," he said.

"Do you like horses?" Jeanette asked eagerly.

"What would a peanut vendor know about horses?" Ajax said. "Hey, Jeanette—watch this."

He ran across the ring and, with a flying leap, landed on his horse's back. Toby watched enviously.

Suddenly Toby said, "I *do* know something about horses. It so happens I got a horse of my own."

Jeanette was delighted. "Really, Toby?"

"Yup. His name is Old Red. Course—he's not really old. That's just his name."

"Is he a gaited horse?"

Toby had never heard the word before. "Gaited?"

"You know—what gait does he favor most?"

"I think he favors the gate most that opens down to the pasture. Lots of sweet clover there."

Jeanette laughed prettily. "Oh, Toby—you're joking."

"Hey, Jeanette!" Ajax called from the ring. "Look!"

He tipped down and did a shoulder stand off the back of his cantering horse.

39

"Gosh," Toby said. "That's pretty good."

Jeanette said, "Don't look at him! He thinks whenever he's out in that ring, the whole world has to stop and watch him. Tell me some more about Old Red. Can he jump?"

"Can he jump!" Toby said. "Like the time he saw a copperhead coiled up in a potato furrow!"

Ajax called again. "Hey, Jeanette!"

This time he unstrapped his leather safety belt and tossed it away with a flourish.

Jeanette turned pale. "Ajax! You know what the colonel said about working without the belt."

Posing cockily, Ajax said, "Aw—who needs that thing? Now that I have your kind attention, I should like to perform that most hazardous of all feats—a genuine somersault!"

Jeanette put her hand up to her mouth. "Ajax, no!"

As Ajax balanced himself for the stunt, several handlers moved forward in alarm. Smiling confidently, the tall boy launched himself forward.

But, instead of completing the somersault, he landed awkwardly on the horse's rump and, losing his balance, crashed heavily to the side of the ring. He lay there with one foot twisted painfully beneath him.

Ben Cotter and Colonel Castle came running. Ben bent down to examine the injury. Shaking his head, he looked up at the colonel. "Pretty bad—"

Ajax was carried off on a stretcher, and Colonel Castle shook his head grimly.

"Here we are," he said, "going into our peak playing time—and a top act goes up the chimney. Well, what do we do about it?"

"Colonel?"

"What?"

"Toby Tyler can ride," Jeanette said.

Ben said, "*Who?*"

Toby gulped. He was more startled than Ben.

"It's true," Jeanette went on earnestly. "He has his own horse at home. He told me."

Toby tried to tiptoe away, but the colonel stopped him with a shout. "*You!* BOY!"

The colonel strode up to where Toby stood quaking. "Can you ride?"

"Me? Well—it was just around the farm—"

"Never mind that. Just so you had *some* experience, I'll take care of the rest!"

Like a drowning man clutching at a straw, Toby said, "But, sir—I've got to work for Mr. Tupper."

The colonel snorted. "I'll take care of Tupper. Now let's get this straight, Toby Tyler. We're going to make a bareback rider out of you! Understand?"

Toby moaned, "Yessir."

The colonel turned to Ben Cotter. "Ben, start first thing tomorrow morning. We'll be at the county seat in Waterford in two weeks. I want this boy riding by then."

In the Ring

Harry Tupper made a long face. He and Colonel Castle were discussing Toby's future. "It's not fair, Colonel," he said gloomily. "Toby Tyler's the best boy I ever had. You can't take him away from me."

"Stop whimpering!" the colonel said. "Find yourself another boy."

"I feel responsible for Toby. He's liable to get hurt fooling around them horses."

"Ben will take good care of him. You know that."

Tupper sighed. "It just don't rest easy on my conscience."

The colonel frowned, and there was a dangerous look in his eye. "Just how much would it take to soothe that conscience of yours?"

"Well—I hate to put it in terms of money—but I'd say, oh, about forty dollars a week."

"Suppose we make it ten."

"How does thirty sound to you, sir?"

"It sounds like fifteen."

"Colonel, I'd like to help you. Tell you what I'll do—"

"No, Mr. Tupper," the colonel shouted. "I'll tell you

what *I'll* do! You get twenty dollars a week finding fee for that boy—and that's final!"

With that agreement, the two men felt they had settled Toby's future. As far as they were concerned, nothing now stood in the way of his becoming a bareback rider. But they didn't know what was going on inside Toby's head.

That night, seated alongside Ben Cotter on the front seat of the monkey wagon, Toby said, "Ben, I told a lie."

Ben nodded gravely. "That so?"

"I can't ride," Toby said. "Not hardly at all."

Ben said, "Ought to be a pretty good pile of coins in that pouch of yours. You could buy a ticket straight home and still have some money to give your Uncle Daniel."

Toby thoughtfully fingered the leather pouch. Mr. Stubbs stirred restlessly on his lap.

"When do you figure on leaving?" Ben said.

"Will you look out for Mr. Stubbs, Ben? He don't know I'm going."

Glaring briefly at the chimp, Ben said, "He won't starve."

"I'll come back some day, Ben, and buy him from Colonel Castle."

"Sure. Now why don't you get some sleep?"

After Toby had settled down on the top of the wagon, he said softly, "Ben—next to Mr. Stubbs, you and Sam are the best friends I got."

"Don't get all wrought up," Ben said. "In a few weeks you'll forget what I looked like."

"No, Ben. I'll never forget you."

"Go to sleep." Ben said.

The caravan continued moving along the road, and at last Toby fell asleep.

But Mr. Stubbs, lying beside him, was still awake and playful. The chimp's paw darted into Toby's pocket and came out with the leather pouch.

Curiously, Mr. Stubbs worked at the drawstring, opened it, and withdrew one of the coins. He sniffed the coin, studied it intently on both sides, and finally bit into it. Then, disappointed by the taste, he heaved it over the side into the passing roadway.

While Toby slept and Ben half dozed on the driver's seat, the chimp kept taking coins out of the pouch. One by one, each coin was sniffed, studied, bitten, and then flung away. When the pouch was empty at last, Mr. Stubbs turned it inside out and, holding it on his lap, went to sleep.

When Toby saw the pouch on the chimp's lap in the morning, he snatched it away and examined it quickly.

"Mr. Stubbs! My money! Where is it?" Toby grabbed the monkey and shook him. "What did you do with it?"

Mr. Stubbs whimpered. Toby had never shaken him before, or spoken in such tones of anger and despair. The chimp tried to climb onto his lap, but Toby pushed him away.

"What's the trouble?" Ben wanted to know.

"Mr. Stubbs threw my money away! That's what I get for making a friend of him!" he said bitterly.

Ben's face grew stern. "Near as I remember," he said, "Colonel Castle made the monk your responsibility. You took him on, didn't you? Nobody forced you to do it?"

Toby bit his lips. "No."

"Then don't go blaming the monk."

"But all my savings! My money is gone."

"You think money's your only problem. That's easy." Ben pulled a wallet out. "Here—take what I've got.

44

There's enough to get you home, and some left over." He pushed some money toward Toby.

Toby's face was flaming. He made no move to take it.

"Take it," Ben said angrily. "And get out of here before you get in any deeper."

Toby remained silent.

Ben rubbed his chin thoughtfully. "You mean you *don't* want to run away?" he said. "You want to go on taking care of this ungrateful little monk?"

Toby pressed his lips together.

"You mean you *want* to go out in the practice ring today and work off some of that trouble you lied yourself into?"

Toby hung his head. He felt, for a moment, as if he were going to cry. Then, suddenly, he reached out and took Mr. Stubbs into his arms.

Ben's eyes twinkled. "All right! See you're in that ring at eleven sharp this morning!" Then he added gruffly, "And don't think it's going to be fun!"

Ben was right; the practice ring wasn't fun.

Toby wore patched tights, with a leather belt around his middle. Attached to the belt was a rope which ran up to an overhead swivel. Ben Cotter stood in the center of the ring, a whip in his hand.

"Go on!" Ben ordered. "Get on the horse! He won't eat you!"

Toby gulped, got on the waiting horse and struggled up to a standing position. Then Ben flicked his whip, and the horse moved forward at a slow walk.

Toby was amazed. The horse had almost completed a full circuit of the ring, and he was still standing. But then Ben flicked his whip again, and the horse's gait changed from a slow walk to a canter.

Immediately Toby lost his balance. The horse shot out from under him and he was left dangling at the end of the safety rope.

Toby floundered in mid air until the horse came around again. Seizing the harness, he pulled himself down onto the horse's back. There he clung, flat on his face.

"Stand up!" Ben shouted.

As the morning wore on, Toby grew wearier and gloomier. "It's no use, Ben!" he said at last. "I can't do it!"

Ben shrugged.

"That's just about what Ajax said would happen."

Toby stuck out his lower lip. "He did, did he?"

"That's not all. Ajax said you'd put your tail between your legs and quit the first day. Well, Toby, was he right? Or are you ready to try again?"

The horse was still circling the ring. Grimly, Toby turned to meet it. He leaped but, hitting the horse's side, bounced away.

Gaining his feet, he turned to meet the horse again. This time he got on top of the animal and managed to pull himself to his feet.

Ben's eyebrows rose. "Not bad for a beginning," he said. "After lunch, we'll work some more."

46

Letters from Home

Day after day, Toby went back to the practice ring. What with Ben's patience, and his own pluck, he was soon standing erect while the horse went around and around the ring at a fast gait.

Harry Tupper was delighted by Toby's rapid progress. The concessionaire loved money above everything else; and he was getting twenty dollars every week from Colonel Castle. His heartfelt wish was that Toby Tyler should be a very good rider and a source of income to him forever.

For Toby, these were the greatest days of his life. But he still thought about home. He couldn't help wondering why he hadn't heard from Uncle Daniel and Aunt Olive; why they hadn't answered his first letter. And so one night, he sat down to write them another letter.

"Ben," he said, "I forgot. How do you spell 'uncle'?"

"Drat it, boy. It's not the spelling of a letter that's important. It's what you say! Did you tell your folks that you missed them?"

"Not exactly," Toby said.

"Did you say you loved them?" Ben continued. "Folks put a lot of store in things like that."

A tear came to Toby's eye. He knew how good it would have made him feel, if his aunt and uncle had written things like that to him. But not even one letter had come from home.

Toby sighed as he wrote the words:

I love you very much.
     Your friend,
     Toby Tyler

The circus reached Waterford a few days later. The street parade had gone smoothly, and now the big show was under way. In less than half an hour, Toby would ride in public for the first time.

Toby's costume, an old cast-off that had once belonged to Ajax, was two sizes too large for him. The reflection staring back at him from the dressing-table mirror looked more like a pale scarecrow than a daring bareback rider.

"You'd be scared too," he said to Mr. Stubbs, who was perched on the table, "if you had to go out in front of all those people!"

At that moment Sam Treat breezed into the tent. "How are we getting on?" the clown said.

Despairingly, Toby tried to gather in some of the slack of the baggy pants. "This doesn't seem to fit very well."

"Ve need some magic," Sam said in his comical Dutch accent. "Close the eyes, blease!"

Toby wonderingly closed his eyes, and Sam beckoned to the entrance flap. A moment later the tent was filled with performers shouting, "Surprise!"

Toby opened his eyes. Jeanette was proudly holding up

a handsome new riding costume directly in front of him.

"It is a gift," she said. "From all of us. Good luck, Toby." The boy's heart brimmed with happiness. He felt that nobody ever had truer friends.

"Everybody out!" Sam shouted. "Toby has just three minutes left to dress."

Toby changed into the new costume with record speed. He looked in the mirror, and smiled proudly.

But then, glancing down at his feet, he groaned. His riding shoes were missing. He had left them at the lemonade stand.

As Toby rushed out, Mr. Stubbs started picking at his tether. The little chimp was an accomplished escape artist. He reached the lemonade stand just a moment after Toby.

There, aping Toby's frantic search for the shoes, he began pawing through the pockets of a coat hanging over a camp chair.

"That's Mr. Tupper's coat!" Toby said. "Leave it!"

Toby found the shoes, then hurried over to pick up some letters that the chimp had dropped to the ground. He was just about to return them to the coat pocket, when suddenly he stopped, frozen, his hand in mid air.

No! Toby thought. It couldn't be. Yet no matter how
he squinted at the envelope, the address remained the same:

Master Toby Tyler
c/o Colonel Castle's Great American Circus

Toby looked at the other envelopes. They were all the
same, all addressed to him, and written by Aunt Olive.

For a moment he was unable to speak or move. Then
he picked up Mr. Stubbs and hugged him.

"They're *all* for me, Mr. Stubbs! They *did* write! They
did!"

Before he could yell another word, or even stop to wonder what the letters had been doing in the pocket of Mr.
Tupper's coat, Ben found him and hauled him off.

In the center ring, Colonel Castle had already started
the announcement:

"Ladies and gentlemen—we present for your kind ap-

proval—those daring young equestrians—Mademoiselle Jeanette and Monsieur Toby!"

Toby was in a daze. But he rode like a veteran, taking all the jumps with ease and grace. The audience clapped and cheered. He and Jeanette had to take repeated bows. And then he had to fight his way through a group of admiring performers.

"Excuse me," he said, stammering his thanks. "I've got to read my letters!"

Back in the tent, Toby removed the letters from inside his riding costume. As he sat down at the dressing table, Mr. Stubbs jumped onto his shoulder.

When Toby had finished reading, his eyes were misted.

"They miss me, Mr. Stubbs," he said softly. "And Uncle Daniel isn't well. He had to take over the chores I used to do—and with the rest of the work, it's too much for him. They want me to come home. They need me. I've got to go to them before anybody here tries to stop me."

Toby quickly changed into his own clothes. He wrote a note saying goodby to Ben and Sam, and put it in the mirror. Then, picking up the chimp, he hugged him tightly.

"Mr. Stubbs," he said, "I can't take you with me. You don't belong to me. They'd say I stole you. You understand, don't you? I'll come back and get you some day. Honest, I will!"

Toby set Mr. Stubbs down and ran out of the tent.

Immediately the little chimp began throwing himself against his tether, trying to break it. He tried again and again, until at last it snapped.

Then he hurried out into the darkness.

51

Pursuit

Unfortunately, it was Harry Tupper who found Toby's note. As he read it, the concessionaire's face grew dark with anger.

The ungrateful little whelp! After all he'd done for him, teaching him the business, then not standing in his way when he wanted to become a bareback rider—!

The boy was a gold mine! To hold onto him, Tupper had tampered with the mails—receiving, reading, and hiding Toby's letters from home. Tupper sighed with desolation.

Then, glancing down, he saw the snapped tether.

Tupper stiffened. The chimp!

A crafty smile slowly spread over his face. The chimp had broken away after the boy. Now Harry Tupper could count on the local sheriff to help get Toby Tyler back.

The chimp caught up with Toby at dawn. The boy was asleep in a culvert, and Mr. Stubbs awakened him by dropping a few sticks on his nose.

"Gosh, Mr. Stubbs," Toby said worriedly. "Why did you follow me? They'll be after me for sure now."

It was still early morning when Harry Tupper, driving a rented one-horse rig, pulled up before a general store not too far from the culvert.

Inside at the counter, a pleasant-faced young man named Jim Weaver was buying cartridges for his rifle. The hunting dog at his feet glanced up as Tupper burst in through the door.

Tupper headed for the telephone on the rear wall, and whirled the side crank importantly. "Operator!" he said. "Get me the sheriff over at Bartonsville. It's important."

At this, Jim Weaver turned and listened attentively.

"Sheriff? This is Harry Tupper, representing Castle's Great American Circus. I want you to look out for a small boy—about eleven years old—calls himself Toby Tyler. I figure he's going in your direction. He ran away last night. Took along a valuable animal. A chimpanzee. Thanks, sheriff. You find him, and we'll be glad to express our appreciation, if you know what I mean."

Tupper was smiling smugly as he hung up. Then, noticing Jim Weaver's rifle and dog, he sauntered over to the counter and addressed the young hunter.

"You probably know this part of the country pretty

well," he said. "If you find that boy—there's a reward of ten dollars in it for you."

Jim Weaver coldly looked Tupper up and down.

"I'm not much at tracking small boys," he said. "Bobcats are fearsome enough for me."

Tupper could sense the distaste Jim Weaver felt for him. He backed away quickly, muttering, "Suit yourself." And then he ran out to the rig and drove away.

Meanwhile, Toby was trudging along the road to Bartonsville, with Mr. Stubbs on his shoulder. The boy's spirits were high, for every step was bringing him closer to his aunt and uncle.

Suddenly there was the sound of an approaching wagon. Quickly, Toby and Mr. Stubbs plunged into the undergrowth at the side of the road.

A few moments later Harry Tupper drove up and stopped. Tupper had spotted a blur of movement as the two had left the road, and now he got down to investigate. He beat through the underbrush, with no success. At last he reluctantly returned to his rig.

Toby and Mr. Stubbs had been hiding behind a tree just beyond the underbrush. As the wagon moved slowly away, they turned and plunged deeper into the woods.

They ran until they came to a softly rolling knoll. Toby felt winded, and slowed down to a walk. Chattering loudly, the chimp scampered ahead and disappeared in the undergrowth.

Nearby, Jim Weaver was instantly alert as his dog stopped in her tracks and pricked up her ears. She had heard Mr. Stubbs. With a yelp, the dog bounded into the bush. The young hunter followed quickly, bringing his rifle to the ready.

54

"Mr. Stubbs!" Toby called. "Where are you? Mr. Stubbs!"

Mr. Stubbs streaked along the ground, closely pursued by the barking dog.

Without breaking his stride, the chimp grabbed an overhanging branch and pulled himself up. Swinging and leaping frantically, he climbed toward the crown of the tree.

Glancing up, Jim Weaver saw some branches moving high overhead. He raised his rifle and took careful aim.

Toby heard the report of the gun, and came running, cold terror on his face.

There was a heavy sound of branches crashing above, and then the little chimp came tumbling through the leaves onto the ground. His eyes were closed and blood was trickling from a wound in his chest. Dropping down beside him, Toby cried out in anguish, "Mr. Stubbs—don't! Don't leave me!"

But the chimp lay motionless, his eyes closed.

Jim Weaver slowly put his rifle down. "Believe me," he said. "I'm sorry. I had no idea. I thought it was a bobcat."

Toby was beyond comforting. "You killed him," he sobbed. "You're a murderer."

Behind them, someone cleared his throat. It was Harry

Tupper. He had heard the barking and the shot, and come running. Now he took in the situation at a glance.

"Well, now, Toby," he said at last. "That's too bad. Really too bad. You see? If you hadn't run away, this terrible thing wouldn't have happened. It's your fault."

Toby was stricken. "My fault?" he said dazedly.

"That's right. Mr. Stubbs would be alive and well now, if you hadn't run off. Come on now—let's go back. Maybe the colonel will give you another pet."

"I want Mr. Stubbs!" Toby sobbed. "I won't leave him!"

But Tupper pulled him roughly to his feet and dragged him away.

"It's not the boy's fault," Jim Weaver said, following them. "It's mine."

Tupper shook his head. "Forget it, young fellow. Accidents will happen. The important thing is, we found the lad safe and sound."

With these words, he pulled the sobbing boy into the rig, and drove off. Jim Weaver stood by the road until the rumble of the wheels faded away. Then he turned and walked back to the place of the accident. As he bent to pick up his rifle, he glanced toward the spot where Mr. Stubbs had fallen.

He gasped, scarcely able to believe his eyes. The little chimp had vanished.

Together Again

The moment the rig pulled into the circus grounds, Toby jumped down and ran toward Colonel Castle's office wagon.

Tupper ran after him shouting, "Just a minute! *I'll* tell him! Stop!"

But Toby was already inside. "Colonel," he said, "it was my fault! I ran away and Mr. Stubbs ran after me! I didn't want it to happen! Honest, I didn't!"

"Toby," the colonel said gently, "there's someone here to see you."

Aunt Olive and Uncle Daniel were sitting in the wagon. Toby's aunt held out her arms, and he ran to her and buried his face in her shoulder.

"Toby," Uncle Daniel said, "will you forgive me?"

Outside, Tupper was being dealt with by Ben Cotter. The strong man's face was grim and forbidding.

"You lily-livered skunk!" he said. "I found out what you did with Toby's letters."

"Now, now, Ben!" Tupper whimpered. "I-I just didn't want to upset the lad."

Ben jabbed him in the chest with his finger, pushing him back.

"Tampering with the mail—that calls for a jail sentence, Mr. Tupper."

"It was just a little tamper," Tupper moaned. "I didn't mean to—I was going to—"

"Would you care to make an agreement, Mr. Tupper?"

"Fine! I'd like that! Anything you say, Ben—"

"I want you to give up the share of Toby's money you've been getting—"

"*Ben!*" The thought of giving up money made Tupper bleat with anguish. "You don't know what you're saying—"

Ben jabbed him in the chest again. "I want you to stay away from that boy—"

"Oh, yes, Ben. Absolutely—"

"I want you to behave nice and pretty—"

"Yessir, Ben! Depend on it! Oh yes, indeed."

"Cause if you don't—I'm liable to do something like this—"

And Ben picked Tupper up by the scruff of the collar and dropped him into a nearby tub of water.

That night Toby walked with his aunt and uncle through the circus grounds.

"You've made a lot of good friends here," Uncle Daniel said.

For a moment Toby said nothing. Then he spoke in a voice so low they could hardly hear the words.

"I just wish you could have met my best friend of all," he said.

Ben Cotter hurried into sight. "Sorry to bother you,